THE FOLLOWERS

Published by Creative Education, Inc., 123 South Broad Street, Mankato, Minnesota 56001. Printed in the United States.

Library of Congress Cataloging in Publication Data

Bunting, Anne Eve.
The followers.

SUMMARY: A fateful encounter with their enemies changes the Tree People's attitude about the Followers.
[1. Rare animals — Fiction] I. Title.
PZ7.B91527Fn [Fic] 78-4921
ISBN 0-87191-627-4

THE FOLLOWERS

Written by Eve Bunting
Illustrated by Don Hendricks

Creative Education

Aspen wakened to hunger. There was always hunger now, and it was hard to remember the last time her stomach had been satisfied.

It was early still, for the second sun had not yet risen from the edge of the horizon. The morning wind rustled the leaves around her nest, making her shiver. The nest was an old one, left here by Tree People who had moved on. It was badly made and held nothing of the comfort of her home nest which was big around as the opening to a cave. Still, she had been lucky to find this one. Some of the Tree People had been forced to spend the night in the crooks of branches or on quickly woven leaf mats, suspended between two limbs.

The High Watcher perched in the treetop above her.

"A quiet night," he called down. "No Followers in sight."

"Good." Aspen looked across and down into the nest where her grandmother slept.

Grandmother was old, so old that she could remember a time when the forest was so big that it took weeks to travel through it, and when the Tree People were as many as the leaves on a full grown oak. Before the Followers came and cut down the trees to shrink their forest.

"They've taken our trees to make their own living places," Aspen had complained yesterday to her friend, Danya. "Why do they hunt us too?"

"It is a long, long time since they took any of our trees," Danya said. "And I think they want to find us, to study us."

"All of us?"

"Not necessarily. Maybe just one or two would do. Remember when Beecher went to find the flock of Cuscos? We'd heard they

laid eggs, sweeter to eat than the eggs of any other bird?"

Aspen nodded.

"So Beecher brought back one Cusco. And its eggs were small and scarcer than the teeth in a sparrow? And we let it go?"

"I remember." Aspen said. "But we're People, not birds. We don't even lay eggs. What can the Followers want with us?"

"The Followers don't know we don't lay eggs. They don't know anything about us. They want to learn." Danya leaned forward. "And we should try to learn about them. To learn their language. It is right that Lan Windflo should be our leader. He is brave and good. But he is not far-seeing. The Tree People are doomed anyway. Our forest has grown too small. Each year there are fewer leaves for winter food. Fewer nuts to store. The old ones tell of the wild celery and cress that used to grow by the ponds. All gone. We are our own enemies. We need..."

Aspen interrupted him. "It is the Followers who are our enemies. And you are crazy to hang above them in the trees, Danya. Just so you can learn their words. One day they'll catch you." She dropped her voice to a whisper. "Tell me what they look like, Danya. Are they really as ugly as the People say?"

"They don't look like us," Danya said. "But that only means that to them, we are ugly."

Aspen sniffed. Danya infuriated her. That was probably why she found herself thinking of him so often. She even dreamed about him.

She'd dreamed of him last night, she remembered now, finger-combing the leaves from her long hair.

In the nest below, her grandmother stirred and sat up.

"Good morning." Aspen swung out of the nest's small warmth and skimmed down the tree trunk, vine flying the narrow space to her grandmother's tree.

A squirrel, disturbed by her landing flicked his bushy tail and called out something insulting. The squirrels and other wild creatures were showing resentment now that there was less forest space and less food for all of them to share.

Aspen's heart sank when she saw how tired her grandmother looked. And her hands had bled in the night. The blood had turned the bark dressing a deeper, darker brown. How was she to swing today on those poor, blistered hands? It's not fair, Aspen thought. The old should be allowed to live peaceably in their own nests. Their forest flying should be gentle, now, slowed with age.

"I saw some berries yesterday, back in that little thicket," she whispered to her grandmother. "They were few and I said nothing then. But now I will go and find them for you."

There was guilt in knowing she'd seen the food and not told the rest of her People. But her first loyalty lay to the needs of her grandmother.

"Wherever you go, go quickly, young Aspen," Lan Windflo called. "And remember, the Followers are just a day's journey back, beyond the pine slope. We must keep moving."

Keep moving where? Aspen wondered as she swung herself back through the trees of yesterday. Danya was right about one thing. Their forest was now too small. Lan had divided the People into seven tribes so that, if they were caught, the Followers would not capture them all. Yet, within the confines of the forest, the tribes kept meeting.

"We should send an emissary to the Followers," Danya had said on the day of the dividing. "Someone to face them and ask them what they want. It would be better than running. Let me try, Lan."

But Lan had said it would be too dangerous.

He would certainly be mad if he knew the chances Danya took, Aspen thought as she gathered the berries. She piled the plump fruit into her bark pouch, resisting the urge to gobble them down herself. There were not many and the grandmother would need them for strength. From time to time she stopped to listen. "Just beyond the pine slope. A day's journey." But still! She was glad that the berry patch ran out when the bark pouch was only half-filled. She pulled the strings closed, and then she heard the noise. It was a slow, earth-shifting noise and she knew instantly what it was. The Followers! They'd been closer than Lan Windflo knew.

Up the nearest tree, climbing higher

and higher, melding herself in the rustlings and shadowings above the path, sitting very still so that her greenness would blend with the leaves and hide her from everything but the blue jay perched beyond her clutching hand.

Then she saw them.

She cowered back, suddenly so frightened that she couldn't breathe. She'd suspected how they would look. Danya had never told her, but others had whispered of their hairiness and their size — small, scary whispers that drifted at night from nest to nest. But imagining and seeing were different.

Each Follower was as large as four Tree People. The hair that covered them was dark brown and thick as the coat of a weasel. As they

Danya has sat above them, she told herself desperately. He has watched them and never been caught.

---

walked they swayed from side to side, like trees in a strong wind. Each one carried a long pole with a noose on the end.

Aspen held herself totally still as they filed below.

Danya has sat above them, she told herself desperately. He has watched them and listened to them and never been caught. If I stay quiet here, and wait....

One massive hand reached down and picked something from the ground.

What?

The pouch! She'd dropped her pouch!

One massive head tilted back to look into the trees.

Had he seen her? Aspen pressed a

hand against her mouth and the movement startled the jay.

"Qua-qua," he screeched and took off in a flash of blue that parted the leaves around her.

One massive hand raised, pointed. Then all the heads tilted upward.

Aspen scrambled to her knees, holding on to the trunk with shaking fingers and shaking toes.

They had seen her.

Careless now of noise she swayed out on the branch and flight jumped to the next one. Don't look below, don't even look, she warned herself. Fear was bitter as bile in her throat. Hide me trees, she whimpered, save me!

She swung through them, her hands finding their own sure holds as she glided in the growth passages. Higher and higher she went, leaving the Followers below, big and cumbersome and earthbound. A breeze of her own making whispered around her. She was lighter than air and suddenly, gloriously sure. They would never catch her! Never! They would never catch any of the People.

And then something sailed through the leaves with a hissing, a burning, and there was a fierceness about her ankle that jerked her to a stop.

She tried to shake free of it, but the fierceness held, and it was pulling her, pulling her through the groaning and the sighing and the crying of the trees to the empty space below.

Falling now, falling.

And something cushioning her before she hit the ground. Someone catching her? Before her parents died, when she was little, her father used to play a game with her and she'd close her eyes and jump from a tall tree to a smaller one, into his waiting arms. But this wasn't her father, and these weren't arms. Something white and soft flowed beneath her, blossomed like a snow flower, and she was held in it, and all was still.

Not even a bird cried in the forest. There was nothing but the whiteness around her and the far away blueness of the sky between the covering trees.

Fear was suffocating her. Because, whatever this was it had to do with the

Followers, and somehow they had caught her. She tried to get up, but the softness held her, and then she saw the ring of faces peering down on her. Brown, hair faces, that blotted out the trees and the sky beyond. Big yellow teeth, showing in snarls or smiles, and then for Aspen there was nothing but darkness.

She was in a clearing with trees all around it. But the trees were dead, laid on top of one another, the leaves and branches cut away so that only the trunks were left. She lay on a flat slab, smooth as a rock but gleaming like the surface of a stream. She couldn't move because of the vines twisted around her ankles and wrists. There were things in the room that she couldn't understand. Big, shining things that stood tall and square and had knots on them, like the knots on a tree trunk. She tried to look at the things in the room instead of at the Followers, but her eyes kept coming back to the huge bodies that surrounded her.

A hairy hand stretched toward her and she tried to edge away. But there was no way to move anything except her head. She turned it to the other side. There were more Followers there. She counted. Eleven, twelve, thirteen that she could see. Now there was a sliding sound. She jerked her head around and saw through the mist of her own terror.

One of the shiny, knobbed things was moving in her direction. Two Followers, one on either side, pushed it. It stopped, towering over her.

One Follower leaned across her. His mouth opened, but the words he spoke meant nothing to her. They were harsh as the grunts of a wildcat, and as frightening.

"Bak-Ad," he said, over and over and over. "Bak-Ad." The eyes that watched her were small and black and sunken under a bristle of brows. He seemed anxious that she understand something. But all she understood was that a shining arm with a fingerless hand was coming closer and closer to her, sliding down from the shine of the tall machine. The fingerless hand hovered over her and she struggled to get away, but the bonds were too tight. Her body was cold with her own sweat.

One Follower laid a heavy hand across her forehead, holding her still.

"Bak-Ad," he grunted.

Sometimes her grandmother held her forehead like that, to comfort her when she was sick. But this was a scratchy thing, rough and coarse as a sandstone rock. Aspen heard herself scream as the other hand, the fingerless one, touched her bare arm, just above her wrist. There was an iciness to it, so cold that it almost burned. She waited for pain, but none came. There was a strange humming noise. As soon as the humming stopped a Follower touched one of the knots, the silver arm lifted and the fingerless hand moved up and away.

Aspen lay absolutely still.

The straps were being loosened. She wanted to close her eyes, to hide from everyone in the room, but if she did close them something awful might happen and she wouldn't see it coming. What would happen next? What else would they do to her? She moved her fingers.

Her hand and arm felt all right. No different.

The Followers watched her intently.

"Can I. . . . get up?" she asked.

"Ta."

What was Ta? Yes? or No?

She slid her shaking legs over the edge of the cold slab. If one of them jumped forward and pushed her back she knew she'd never again have the courage to try to stand.

A Follower gripped her elbow. He was helping her. Helping her! She was dizzy and she stood holding on to his hairy arm.

Another Follower bowed and made a sweeping motion toward the opening between the piled up logs. Another held something out to her, something that looked small on his huge, black palm. Her berry pouch! Aspen's hand shook

Outside now, out and running, running through the clearing and beyond.

---

as she took it. He grunted something and pointed to the sun filled opening. The others stood aside, leaving a passageway for her to walk through.

"You mean...I can leave? I'm free?" Aspen whispered. "That's all? That's all you wanted?"

The sweeping motion came again.

Aspen stumbled weakly toward the shaft of sunlight.

Outside now, out and running, running through the clearing to the trees beyond. She jumped for a low branch and began climbing. Free! Free! She couldn't believe it.

Once she glanced back and saw the group of Followers standing by the piled up logs, watching her go. Their lifted hands shaded their eyes from the white light of the second sun. It was as if they waved her goodbye.

Aspen leaped from tree to tree. Ahead were her People. Her mind circled around what had happened to her. Would the Followers go away now? She felt like a bird, a Cusco bird, winging to freedom. Danya said there were things the Followers wanted to know. Had they learned from her that the People didn't lay eggs, or spin webs, or sting, or change colors like chameleons? Had the magic of the fingerless hand that buzzed told them all those things?

Lan Windflo didn't understand it either. None of the people did when she told them what had happened.

"But you were gone such a short time," Lan said. "We had just realized that you were missing."

"If she knew their language she could have asked them what they were doing." Danya said. "Maybe we have no need to be afraid. You should have tried to talk to them, Aspen."

Aspen stared at him. What did he know of the terror? Talk to them, indeed!

The People crowded around her to

examine the place above her wrist. But there was nothing to see and nothing to feel.

"Sometimes a Tree Person will put a mark on a tree or nest to show that it belongs to him," Lan said. "But that makes no sense. And there is no mark unless it is visible to their eyes and not ours."

Aspen's grandmother touched her hair. "You are safe," she said. "That is all that matters."

They posted two High Watchers that night and again the next, and they kept moving, putting distance between themselves and the place of the Followers.

On the third day the far High Watcher swung in to report that the Followers were leaving the forest.

The People smiled at each other uncertainly.

"Can it be true?" they asked. "Has it ended?"

Aspen felt their loving concern as she answered their questions. Yes, she felt fine. She didn't feel anything different. But Lan's words about the ownership mark on a tree or nest haunted her. She couldn't belong to the Followers now, could she?

Lan decided that for now they should stay away from the home nests and that the seven tribes should remain separate.

On the twelfth day that was free from Followers he climbed to the highest tree top and blew on his bone horn. The note echoed around the forest, bounced from the trees, lay sweetly in the shadowed clearings. It was the signal for safety.

With joy the tribes blocked back to the home nests and there was unity again in the forest.

"Now we are safe to die slowly of starvation," Danya said grimly.

"Better than being captured by those ...those...." Aspen told him. The memory of the fingerless hand began to dull for her. Had it really happened? Or was it only a dream?

It was thirty days before the Followers struck.

Deep night, and the twin moons hidden behind a covering of misty clouds.

Aspen wakened with a start to a loud, regular clicking sound. She sat up in her nest, frightened by the strangeness of this alien sound in the stillness of the summer night. The clicking was in her nest, here, beside her. What was it? Too loud to be a snake. Too loud to be anything living.

Someone called from the nest next to hers.

"What is that? What is the noise?"

Horrified, Aspen realized that *she* was clicking, the sound was coming from her body, from deep inside her. She held up her hand. It was coming from the place above her wrist where the fingerless thing had touched her skin.

"Grandmother!" she yelled. "Danya! Lan!" She rubbed at the ticking place, clamped her other hand tightly over it, but the sound came through.

"Aspen?" It was Danya's voice coming from the darkness, and then there was no more darkness. Lights speared down from the sky, lights brighter than the mid time glare of the double suns, and there was a humming and a dark, black shadow hanging just above the lights.

"What. . . ." Aspen shaded her eyes and stared up. The dark shadow was a giant bird creature, its wing span stretching wider than a hundred trees, but it wasn't alive, she knew that. It had been made by the Followers, the way the shining thing with the fingerless hand had been made.

All around her the People sat up in their nests, dazzled and confused by the lights and the noise.

"Out! Out of the nests! Get away!" Lan yelled.

But it was too late.

Something was dropping from the black sky shadow, something like a giant, glittering cobweb.

The People swarmed down the tree trunks, tried to vine-swing themselves to safety. But the cobwebs fell like rain, covering the nests and the trees and the People.

Aspen pulled at the one that encased her nest, trying to tear it away. But there was a stickiness in the web's shine, like fresh tree sap, and it clung to her hands where she touched it, imprisoning her. The more she struggled, the worse it became. Now her arms were caught too and one of her legs. Like a fly, she thought, terrified, and she forced herself to be still, hearing the terrible clicking that came from her and that went on and on and on through the screams and the sobbings around her. All of the People were trapped. It seemed as if none had escaped. Some had struggled so desperately that their bodies were wound in the webs, wrapped like chrysalises in sticky cocoons.

Then, in a shaft of light, Aspen saw the Followers.

They shambled beneath the trees, squinting up against the lights, talking amongst themselves in those harsh, ugly voices. Inspecting the People, trapped above them.

One Follower carried something that shone and clicked with the same click that came from Aspen's wrist. He stopped under her tree and held up the fingerless hand. The clicking was unbearably loud now, joined exactly to hers, the two hearts beating together. Then both clickings stopped and there was only the hum of the shadow in the sky and the moans of the People.

Now she understood. The understanding brought so much despair that she felt numb. They *had* put something invisible on her skin. A sound. And the sound had led them directly to her, and to her People. In a way she *had* belonged to them all this time. And they had been so clever. They had waited, to make the people feel secure enough to come together. This way they could capture all of them in one swoop. She felt the trickle of tears on her cheeks and she tried to free a hand to wipe them away. But her hand was trapped. Unchecked, the tears ran salty into her mouth.

As if he read her thoughts Lan spoke from the mesh of his web. "It isn't any fault of yours, Aspen. Any one of us could have been taken. Any one of us could have led them here."

Whatever else he said was drowned in the roar that came from the giant shadow above them. It was dropping, hanging now just over the tops of the tallest trees. The cobweb

traps sparkled in the lights. The fine, shining threads that held them to the shadow disappeared above into the darkness.

One of the Followers on the ground raised both arms, spread them wide, then raised them again over his head.

Aspen felt an upward tug on her web, a lifting.

She tried to reach for the tree trunk, to hold on to it, but her prison held her too tightly.

Up, up, up.

Her tree seemed to reach out its branches to hold her, but its efforts were useless as her own.

Now she dangled in the web, high above everything, and all around her were her People, dangling singly or in family nets of two or three or four. She swung gently, turning slowly in lazy circles. She saw her grandmother. The mesh had tangled round her shoulders and draped itself across her back. And Danya? Where was he?

The night was filled with the cries of

the People, calling to one another in frightened voices.

"Don't struggle," a man's voice urged. "The stickiness is strong. But we don't know how much strain it will take."

Aspen glanced down and shuddered. No, don't struggle. Don't free yourself now, to fall into that emptiness below. But falling might be better than whatever lay in store for them.

The big, dark shadow hummed quietly through the softness of the night. It was eerie to see the world from here. Aspen looked down upon their forest and saw the smallness of it, the bald patches between the trees. Just beyond lay the Followers' living places. The sky bird lights picked out shelters made from cut down trees, and others that shone cold and silver, and still others standing straight and tall and smooth as cliffs. Paths zig-zagged between the living places, wide paths, and she could see dark spots that might be Followers standing in groups. She imagined them staring up into the night sky, pointing at the People dangling in their shining

To plunge into that deep, cold darkness, to be pulled down, down, down, into the dreadful depths.

---

webs. Did all the Followers know about the trap that had been set for the Tree People? Did they know what was to happen to them at the end of this nightmare ride in the sky?

They had gone past the living places now and below lay a great pond, the water gleaming smooth as black ice.

Aspen curled her fingers around the stickiness of the web. To fall here! To plunge into that deep, cold darkness, to be pulled down, down, down into the dreadful depths!

But now there were trees below. The forest stretched endlessly ahead and to the side, as far as Aspen could see. There was a thickness, a closed-over greenness that blended the treetops together so that they looked soft as the moss on a river rock.

To fall here might be possible. If the hands could grasp a branch in the falling, if the moss-trees would cushion the crash.

There was a clearing, an open space in the density of the forest, wide as a meadow but gleaming with a strange whiteness.

The shadow hovered, then began slowly to drop.

Lower and lower.

Whiteness, and dark figures.

The shadow sound changed to a low hum, and then there was the sudden awfulness of falling, the air whistling around her, worse,

worse than it had been on the day of the catching when they'd pulled her from the tree. Screams around her, and herself screaming, and a flash of knowledge that the sky shadow had cast off the threads that held the webs to it. Then there was green spinning past her, and she was somersaulting, bouncing gently and effortlessly in the whiteness, bouncing and at last lying still.

The whiteness surged as others landed on it, soft as snow, and immense. One body falling after another, almost in a line. Danya! Danya was close to her, and no time to see if the grandmother was safely down because air was blowing on her, warm air with a strange perfume, and it was coming on to her body in a stream, like water.

The web was dissolving around her, coming away in shreds, shrivelling the way autumn leaves shrivelled, turning into dust that lay in small piles that blew with each breath of air against the surrounding whiteness.

Aspen lay, seeing the dark shadow that had brought them to this place move away a little, seeing the yellow circle of the moon twin show itself for an instant between the clouds and disappear again. The lights slanted now at an angle, and Aspen lifted her head and saw Followers all around them.

Hairy arms reached out, helping them come off the whiteness and stand.

Aspen saw her grandmother. She stumbled to her and put an arm around the thin, old shoulders.

"Are you all right, Grandmother? Did you get hurt in the fall?"

"I'm not hurt. The whiteness was soft enough for even my aging bones."

They stood, all of them, caught in the circles of light. On either side the forest stretched invitingly.

Aspen stared around. Wide circles of chopped down trees dotted the clearing and she saw that they were covered with leaves on which were piled nuts and berries and pale white strips of celery and rich, brown, tender roots. There were mounds of feathery green and she saw the soft creaminess of the fungus that was now so rare in their forest that it was kept for special

days. In spite of her fear she heard her stomach growl and felt the saliva juices spurt into her mouth.

"Bak-Ad," a Follower said. He gestured to the food.

Lan's voice came from somewhere in the mass of shivering People. "When I give the signal, run. Take to the trees."

"Wait! 'Bak-Ad' means 'we will not hurt you'. Or perhaps, 'do not be afraid'. I've heard them use these words to calm a frightened wild creature."

It was the word they'd said to her, Aspen remembered. On the night of the catching.

Danya stepped in front of the Followers. Follower sounds, slow and hesitant came from his mouth. The Followers lips lifted over their teeth in what might have been smiles and she heard them answer him.

There was a chance to run now. But instead, the People just stood still. Lan gave no signal.

Danya's eyes were shining. "I understand only a little. But it is enough. They brought us here because we are so few. They are afraid we are endangered, that we may be lost to the planet for ever. This forest will be better for us. There is food here and the warmth and shelter of many trees. It is to be our new home. And they are sorry that in times past they took so many of our forest's trees. Here it will be different."

"You mean we are free? Free to go?"

"Yes. They invite us first to eat. If we want to."

No one stopped to eat, though Aspen knew that hunger gnawed in them as fiercely as it did in her. One by one and two by two, with backward glances, the People moved slowly into the comfort of the trees.

A Follower stepped toward Aspen. He held something in his hand that caught and reflected the light from the sky. Fear jumped in Aspen's throat as he caught her arm and pressed the glowing thing against the signal place.

"Fasel," he grunted and spread his arms wide.

"I think he means that it is finished," Danya said. "There will be no more signal sounds and no more need for them."

Aspen nodded. She'd known herself what he said. And what he meant.

"How do I tell him 'thank-you'?" she asked.

"Pel ton."

Aspen looked up into the dark eyes under the bristle of brows. There was kindness there, understanding too, if you looked closely and without fear.

"Pel ton," she said.

"Pel ton." Lan Windflo echoed quietly, and then he and Danya and the grandmother and Aspen walked together into the welcoming forest.

The Space People
The Undersea People
Day of the Earthlings
The Robot People
The Mirror Planet
The Island of One
The Followers
The Mask